KU-229-482

بَدَأَهَا الثَّعْلَبُ عِنْدَمَا دَعَا طَائِرَ الكُرْكِيِّ إِلى العَشَاءِ ...

عِنْدَمَا وَصَلَ طَائِرُ الكُرْكِيِّ إِلى بَيْتِ الثَّعْلَبِ رَأَى أَطْبَاقاً مِنْ كُلِّ الأَلْوانِ وَالأَشْكالِ

مَصْفُوفَةً عَلَى الرُّفُوفِ ؛ ومِنها أَطْبَاقٌ كَبِيرَةٌ وطَوِيلَةٌ وضَيِّقَةٌ وصَغِيرَةٌ.

وكَانَ عَلَى الطَّاوِلَةِ طَبَقَانِ مُسَطَّحَانِ مُنْبَسِطانِ.

حَاوَلَ طَائِرُ الكُرْكِيِّ أَنْ يَنْقُرَ وَيَلْقُطَ الحَسَاءَ بِمِنْقَارِهِ الطَّوِيلِ النَّحِيفِ. لَكِنْ،
بِالرُّغْمِ مِنْ جَمِيعِ المُحَاوَلَاتِ لَمْ يَسْتَطِعْ أَنْ يَرْشُفَ رَشْفَةً وَاحِدَةً مِنَ الحَسَاءِ.

  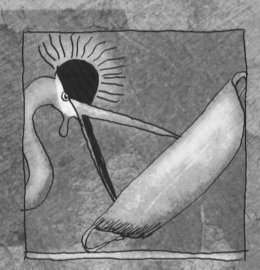

Crane pecked and she picked with her long thin beak. But no matter
how hard she tried she could not get even a sip of the soup.

الثَّعْلبُ وَطائرُ الكُرْكِيِّ

خُرافةٌ لِ " أَيْسوب "

The Fox and the Crane

- an Aesop's Fable

retold by Dawn Casey

illustrated by Jago

Arabic translation by Wafa' Tarnowska

Bromley Libraries

30128 80282 749 6

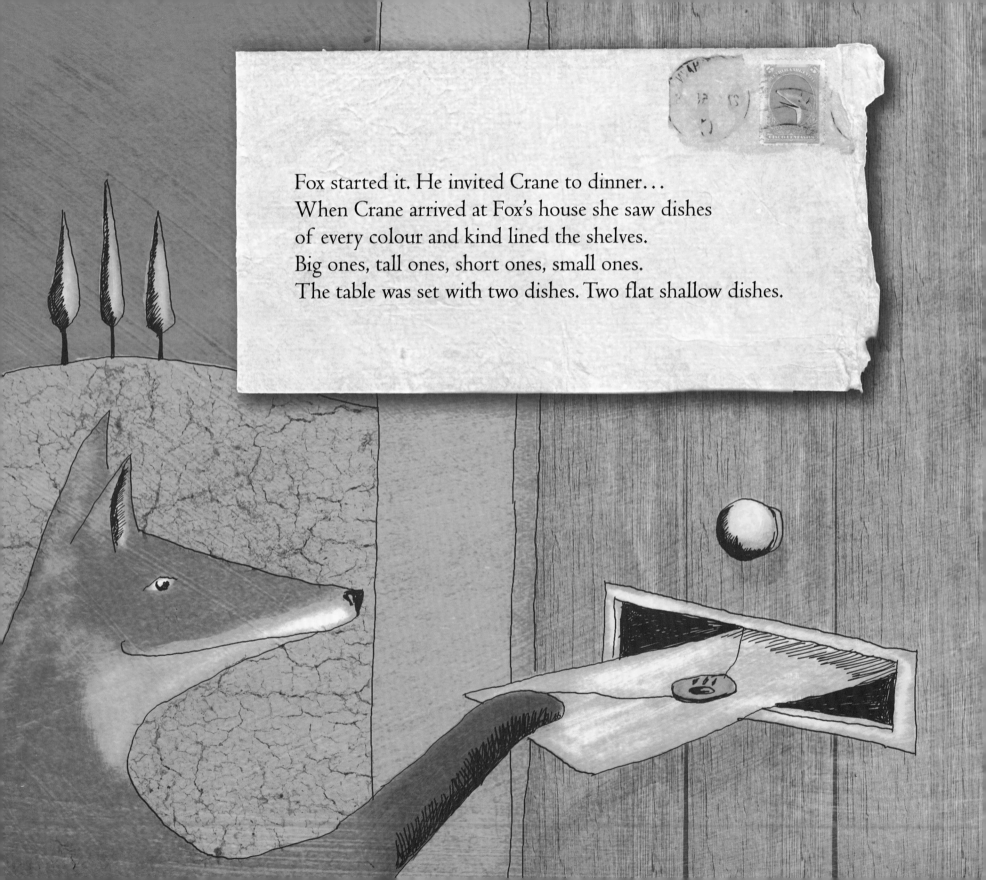

Fox started it. He invited Crane to dinner…
When Crane arrived at Fox's house she saw dishes
of every colour and kind lined the shelves.
Big ones, tall ones, short ones, small ones.
The table was set with two dishes. Two flat shallow dishes.

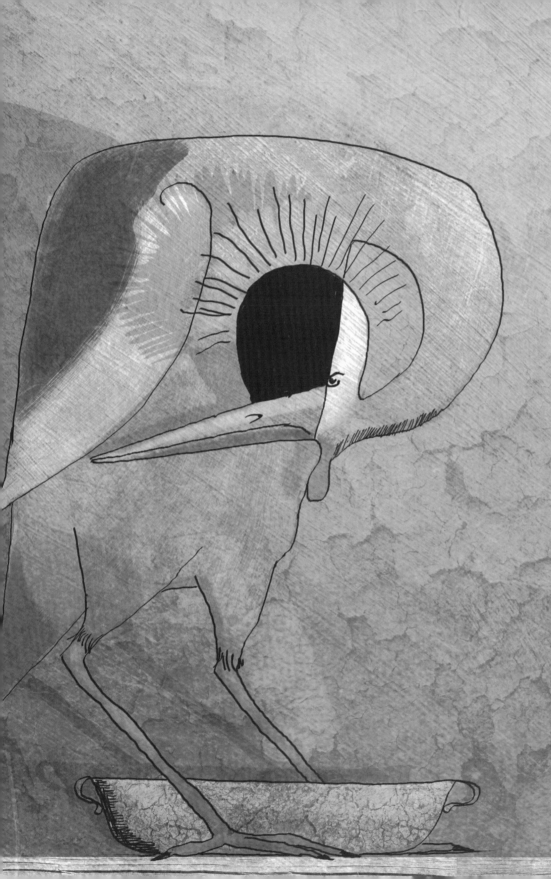

كَانَ الثَّعْلَبُ يُرَاقِبُ مُجَاهَدَةَ الكُرْكِيِّ سَاخِرًا.

ثُمَّ رَفَعَ صَحْنَ الحَسَاءِ إِلَى شَفَتَيْهِ وابْتَلَعَهُ

رَشْفَةً شَرْبَةً جَرْعَةً.

"آهِ مَا أَطْيَبَهُ!" قَالَ الثَّعْلَبُ هَازِئًا.

ثُمَّ مَسَحَ شَارِبَيْهِ بِكَفِّهِ وَأَضَافَ مُبْتَسِمًا:

"أَيُّهَا الكُرْكِيُّ لَمْ تَذُقْ حَسَاءَكَ.

إِنَّنِي آسِفٌ أَنَّكَ مَا أَحْبَبْتَهُ،"

قَالَ ذَلِكَ مُحَاوِلاً أَنْ لا يَضْحَكَ عَلَنًا.

Fox watched Crane struggling and sniggered.
He lifted his own soup to his lips, and with
a SIP, SLOP, SLURP he lapped it all up.
"Ahhhh, delicious!" he scoffed, wiping his
whiskers with the back of his paw.
"Oh Crane, you haven't touched your soup,"
said Fox with a smirk. "I AM sorry you
didn't like it," he added, trying not to snort
with laughter.

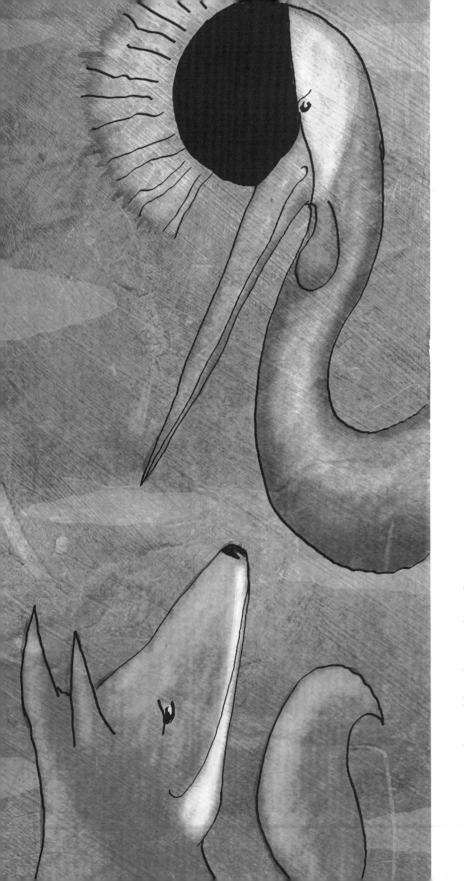

لَمْ يَقُلْ طَائِرُ الكُرْكِيِّ شَيْئًا. نَظَرَ إِلى طَعامِهِ.
نَظَرَ إِلى طَبَقِهِ. نَظَرَ إِلى الثَّعْلَبِ
وَتَبَسَّمَ ثُمَّ قال بِكُلِّ تَهْذيبٍ: "عَزيزي الثَّعْلَبُ،
أَشْكُرُكَ عَلى لُطْفِكَ. اسمَحْ لي أَنْ أَرُدَّ لَكَ الجَميلَ.
تَفَضَّلْ عِنْدي لِلْعَشاءِ."
عِنْدَما وَصَلَ الثَّعْلَبُ إِلى بَيْتِ الكُرْكِيِّ
كَانَ الشُّبّاكُ مَفْتُوحًا. كَانَتْ رَائِحَةٌ ذَكِيَّةٌ تَنْبَعِثُ مِنْهُ.
رَفَعَ الثَّعْلَبُ خَطْمَهُ وَشَمْشَمَ فَسالَ لُعابُهُ وَقَرْقَرَتْ مَعِدَتُهُ
وَلَحَسَ شَفَتَيْهِ.

Crane said nothing. She looked at the meal. She looked
at the dish. She looked at Fox, and smiled.
"Dear Fox, thank you for your kindness," said Crane
politely. "Please let me repay you – come to dinner at
my house."

When Fox arrived the window was open. A delicious
smell drifted out. Fox lifted his snout and sniffed. His
mouth watered. His stomach rumbled. He licked his lips.

"عَزِيزِي الثَّعْلَبُ، تَفَضَّلْ،" قَالَ طَائِرُ الكُرْكِيِّ
بَاسِطًا جَنَاحَيْهِ بِبَشَاشَةٍ.
دَفَعَهُ الثَّعْلَبُ جَانِبًا وَدَخَلَ.
رَأَى أَطْبَاقًا مِنْ كُلِّ الأَشْكَالِ وَالأَلْوَانِ
مَصْفُوفَةً عَلَى الرُّفُوفِ
ومنها أَطْبَاقٌ حَمْرَاءَ وزَرْقَاءَ وقَدِيمَةٌ وَجَدِيدَةٌ.
وكَانَ عَلَى الطَّاوِلَةِ طَبَقَانِ طَوِيلانِ رَفِيعانِ.

"My dear Fox, do come in," said Crane,
extending her wing graciously.
Fox pushed past. He saw dishes of
every colour and kind lined the shelves.
Red ones, blue ones, old ones, new ones.
The table was set with two dishes.
Two tall narrow dishes.

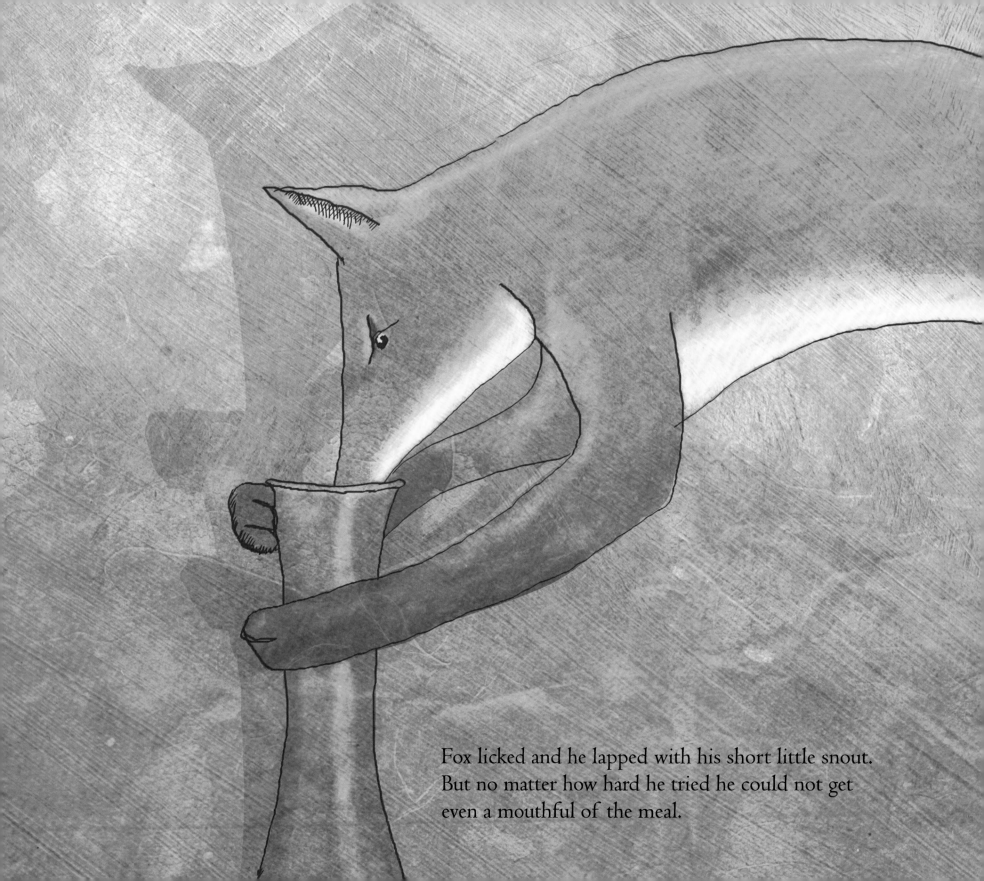

Fox licked and he lapped with his short little snout. But no matter how hard he tried he could not get even a mouthful of the meal.

أَخَذَ الثَّعْلَبُ يَلْحَسُ ويَلْعَقُ الْحَسَاءَ بِخَطْمِهِ الْقَصِيرِ الْعَرِيضِ.
لَكِنْ بِالرُّغْمِ مِنْ جَمِيعِ الْمُحَاوَلاتِ لَمْ يَسْتَطِعْ أَنْ يَأْكُلَ لُقْمَةً
وَاحِدَةً مِنْ هَذا الطَّعامِ.

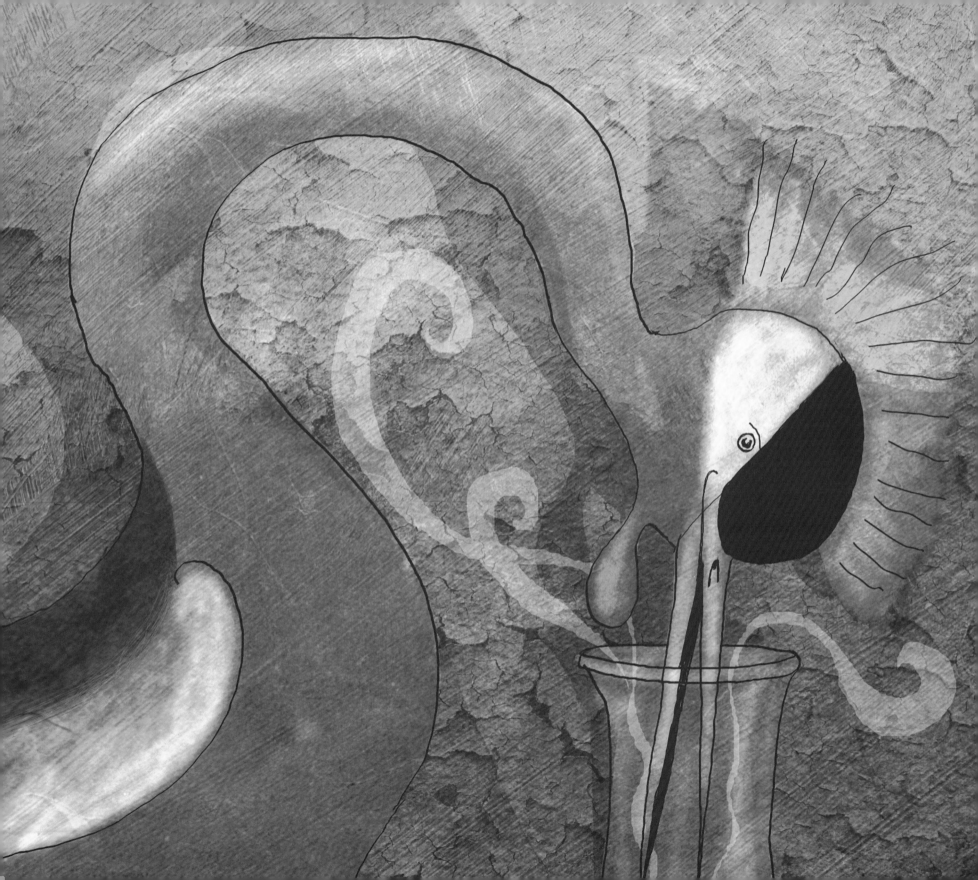

أَكَلَ طَائِرُ الكُرْكِيِّ عَشَاءَهُ بِبُطْءٍ شَدِيد مُتَلَذِّذًا بِكُلِّ لُقْمَةٍ، ثُمَّ تَبَسَّمَ وَقَالَ:
"عَزِيزِي الثَّعْلَبُ أَشْكُرُكَ عَلى زِيَارَتِكَ. لَقَدْ سُرِرْتُ أَنْ أَرُدَّ لَكَ الجَمِيلَ".

أَخَذَتْ مَعِدَةُ الثَّعْلَبِ تُقَرْقِرُ وتُهَمْهِمُ.
وَعِنْدَمَا عَادَ إِلى بَيْتِهِ كَانَ مَا يَزَالُ جَائِعًا.

Crane ate her meal very slowly, savouring every mouthful.
"Dear Fox, thank you so much for coming," she smiled,
"it has been a pleasure to repay your kindness."

Fox's tummy gurgled and grumbled.
And when he went home, he was still hungry.

The Fox and the Crane

Writing Activity:
Read the story. Explain that we can write our own fable by changing the characters.

Discuss the different animals you could use, bearing in mind what different kinds of dishes they would need! For example, instead of the fox and the crane you could have a tiny mouse and a tall giraffe.

Write an example together as a class, then give the children the opportunity to write their own. Children who need support could be provided with a writing frame.

Art Activity:
Dishes of every colour and kind! Create them from clay, salt dough, play dough… Make them, paint them, decorate them…

Maths Activity:
Provide a variety of vessels: bowls, jugs, vases, mugs… Children can use these to investigate capacity:

Compare the containers and order them from smallest to largest.

Estimate the capacity of each container.

Young children can use non-standard measures e.g. 'about 3 beakers full'.

Check estimates by filling the container with coloured liquid ('soup') or dry lentils.

Older children can use standard measures such as a litre jug, and measure using litres and millilitres. How near were the estimates?

Label each vessel with its capacity.

The King of the Forest

Writing Activity:
Children can write their own fables by changing the setting of this story. Think about what kinds of animals you would find in a different setting. For example how about 'The King of the Arctic' starring an arctic fox and a polar bear!

Storytelling Activity:
Draw a long path down a roll of paper showing the route Fox took through the forest. The children can add their own details, drawing in the various scenes and re-telling the story orally with model animals.

If you are feeling ambitious you could chalk the path onto the playground so that children can act out the story using appropriate noises and movements! (They could even make masks to wear, decorated with feathers, woollen fur, sequin scales etc.)

Music Activity:
Children choose a forest animal. Then select an instrument that will make a sound that matches the way their animal looks and moves. Encourage children to think about musical features such as volume, pitch and rhythm. For example a loud, low, plodding rhythm played on a drum could represent an elephant.

Children perform their animal sounds. Can the class guess the animal?

Children can play their pieces in groups, to create a forest soundscape.

ملكُ الغابَةِ

" خُرافَةٌ مِنَ الصِّينِ "

The King of the Forest
- a Chinese Fable

retold by Dawn Casey

illustrated by Jago

Arabic translation by
Wafa' Tarnowska

كَانَ الثَّعْلَبُ يَمْشي في الغابَةِ عِنْدَمَا سَمِعَ شَيْئًا يَتَحَرّكُ بَيْنَ الأَعْشابِ الطَّويلَةِ،

حَفيفَ شَيْءٍ كَبيرٍ،

وَميضَ شَيْءٍ عَيْناهُ صَفْراوانِ،

بَريقَ شَيْءٍ أَسْنانُهُ مِثْلُ السَّكَاكينِ.

Fox was walking in the forest when he heard something moving in the long grass.

RUSTLE   Something big.

BLINK   Something with yellow eyes.

FLASH   Something with teeth like knives.

"صَبَاحُ الخَيْرِ أَيُّها الثَّعْلَبُ الصَّغِيرُ،" قَالَ النَّمِرُ مُبْتَسِمًا وكَانَ فَمُهُ مُمْتَلِئًا أَسْنَانًا.

بَلَعَ الثَّعْلَبُ رِيقَهُ.

"إِنَّني مَسْرُورٌ بِمَعْرِفَتِكَ،" قَالَ النَّمِرُ مُخرْخِرًا. "لَقَدْ بَدَأْتُ أَشعُرُ بِالجُوعِ."

فَكَّرَ الثَّعْلَبُ بِسُرْعَة ثُمَّ قَالَ: "كَيْفَ تَتَجاسَرُ عَلَيَّ! أَلا تَعْلَمُ أَنَّني مَلِكُ الغَابَةِ؟"

"أَنْتَ مَلِكُ الغَابَةِ ؟" أَجَابَ النَّمِرُ وَزَمْجَرَ ضَاحِكًا.

"إِذَا لَمْ تُصَدِّقْني،" قَالَ الثَّعْلَبُ، "سِرْ وَرائِي وسَوْفَ تَرَى أَنَّ الجَمِيعَ يَخَافُ مِنِّي."

"يَجِبُ أَنْ أَرَى هَذا كَي أُصَدِّقَهُ،" قَالَ النَّمِرُ.

بَدَأَ الثَّعْلَبُ يَمْشِي في الغَابَةِ والنَّمِرُ وَرَاءَهُ مُتَكَبِّرًا وذَنبُهُ عَالٍ،

إِلى أَنْ سَمِعا...

"Good morning little fox," Tiger grinned, and his mouth was nothing but teeth.
Fox gulped.
"I am pleased to meet you," Tiger purred. "I was just beginning to feel hungry."
Fox thought fast. "How dare you!" he said. "Don't you know I'm the King of the Forest?"
"You! King of the Forest?" said Tiger, and he roared with laughter.
"If you don't believe me," replied Fox with dignity, "walk behind me and you'll see –
everyone is scared of me."
"This I've got to see," said Tiger.
So Fox strolled through the forest. Tiger followed behind proudly, with his tail held high,
until…

نَعيقاً!

إنَّهُ صَقْرٌ كَبيرٌ ذو مِنْقارٍ أَعْقَفَ. أَلْقَى الصَّقْرُ نَظرَةً

واحِدةً عَلى النَّمِرِ ورَفْرَفَ بِجَناحَيْه طائرًا نَحْوَ الأَشْجارِ.

"هَلْ تَرَى؟" قالَ الثَّعْلبُ. "الجَميعُ يَخافُ مِنِّي!"

"هَذا شَيْءٌ لا يُصَدَّقُ!" أَجابَ النَّمرُ.

وتَابَعَ الثَّعْلبُ سَيْرَهُ في الغَابةِ وَالنَّمِرُ يَتْبَعُهُ بِخِفَّةٍ

وذَنَبُهُ مُسْتَرْخٍ بَعْضَ الشَّيْءِ

إِلى أَنْ سَمِعَا...

SQUAWK!
A huge hook-beaked hawk! But the hawk took
one look at Tiger and flapped into the trees.
"See?" said Fox. "Everyone is scared of me!"
"Unbelievable!" said Tiger.
Fox strode on through the forest.
Tiger followed behind lightly,
with his tail drooping slightly,
until…

هَرِيراً!

إنَّهُ دُبٌّ كَبِيرٌ أَسْوَدُ! لَكِنَّ الدُّبَّ أَلْقَى نَظْرَةً وَاحِدَةً عَلى النَّمِرِ

وَغَابَ في الأَدْغَالِ.

"هَلْ تَرَىْ؟" قَالَ الثَّعْلَبُ. "الجَمِيعَ يَخَافُ مِنِّي."

"هَذا شَيْءٌ لا يُصَدَّقُ!" أَجَابَ النَّمِرُ.

وَمَشى الثَّعْلَبُ في الغَابَةِ وَالنَّمِرُ يَتْبَعُهُ وَذَنَبُهُ يَجُرُّ عَلى أَرْضِ الغَابَةِ
إِلى أَنْ سَمِعَا...

GROWL!
A big black bear! But the bear took one look
at Tiger and crashed into the bushes.
"See?" said Fox. "Everyone is scared of me!"
"Incredible!" said Tiger.
Fox marched on through the forest. Tiger
followed behind meekly, with his tail
dragging on the forest floor, until...

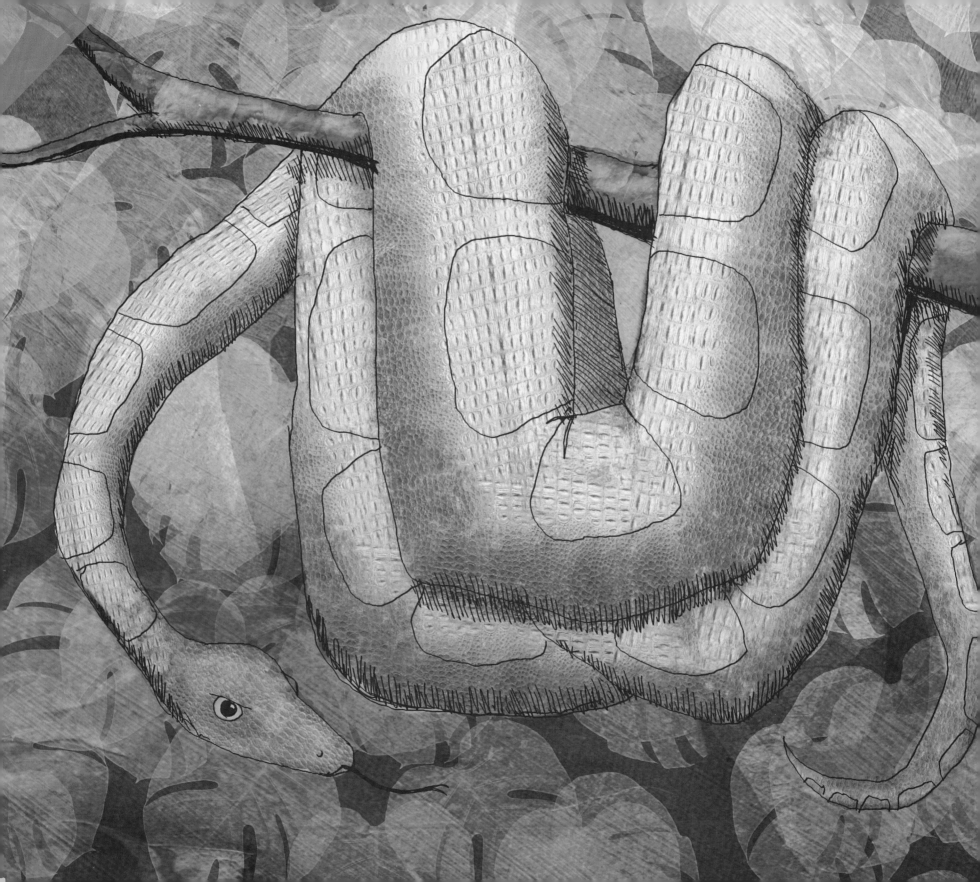

هَسِيساً!

إنَّهُ ثُعْبَانٌ يَنْسِلُّ زَاحِفًا!

لَكِنَّ الثُّعْبَانَ أَلْقَى نَظْرَةً وَاحِدَةً عَلى النَّمِرِ وَانْزَلَقَ نحْوَ الهَشيرِ.

"هَل تَرى؟" قَالَ الثَّعْلَبُ. "الجَميعُ يَخافُ مِنِّي!"

HISSSSSSS!
A slinky slidey snake! But the snake took one look
at Tiger and slithered into the undergrowth.
"SEE?" said Fox. "EVERYONE IS SCARED
OF ME!"

"I do see," said Tiger, "you are the King of the Forest and I am your humble servant."
"Good," said Fox. "Then, be gone!"

And Tiger went, with his tail between his legs.

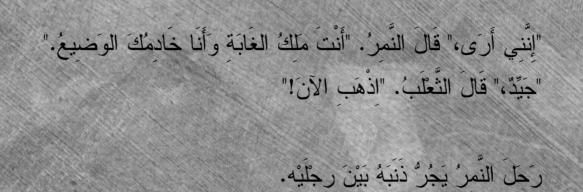

"إِنَّنِي أَرَى،" قَالَ النَّمِرُ. "أَنْتَ مَلِكُ الغَابَةِ وَأَنَا خَادِمُكَ الوَضِيعُ."

"جَيِّدٌ،" قَالَ الثَّعْلَبُ. "اذْهَبِ الآنَ!"

رَحَلَ النَّمِرُ يَجُرُّ ذَنَبَهُ بَيْنَ رِجْلَيْهِ.

"مَلَكُ الغابةِ،" قالَ الثَّعْلَبُ لنَفْسِه مُبْتَسِمًا. وتَحوَّلَت ابْتِسامَتُهُ إلى تَكْشِيرَةٍ وتَحوَّلَتِ
التَّكْشِيرَةُ إِلى كَرْكَرَةٍ وظَلَّ يَضْحَكُ بِصوْتٍ عَالٍ إِلى أَنْ وَصَلَ إِلى بَيْتِهِ.

"King of the Forest," said Fox to himself with a smile. His smile grew into a grin,
and his grin grew into a giggle, and Fox laughed out loud all the way home.

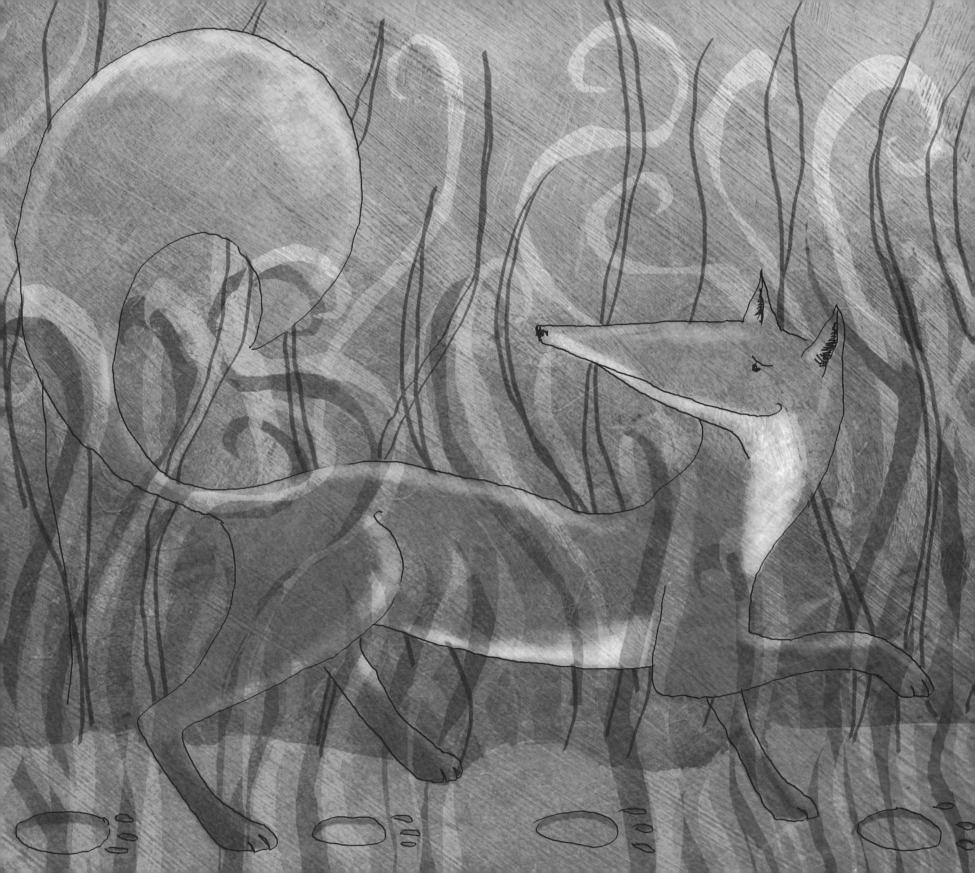

To my Nana, with love ~ DC

For my wife, Alex ~ J

First published in 2006 by Mantra Lingua Ltd
Global House, 303 Ballards Lane
London N12 8NP
www.mantralingua.com

Text copyright © 2006 Dawn Casey
Illustration copyright © 2006 Jago
Dual language copyright © 2006 Mantra Lingua Ltd
This edition 2012

All rights reserved

A CIP record for this book is available from the British Library